Spooky MAZES

CLEVER Publishing

Treasure Hunt

Help the zombie get to the treasure chest at the top of the mountain. Don't forget to grab the key on the way!

FINISH

START

Witch's Brew

Guide the witch through the swampy maze to reach the cauldron.

START

FINISH

Swamp Searching

The witch needs four spiders to make a potion. Can you help her find them?

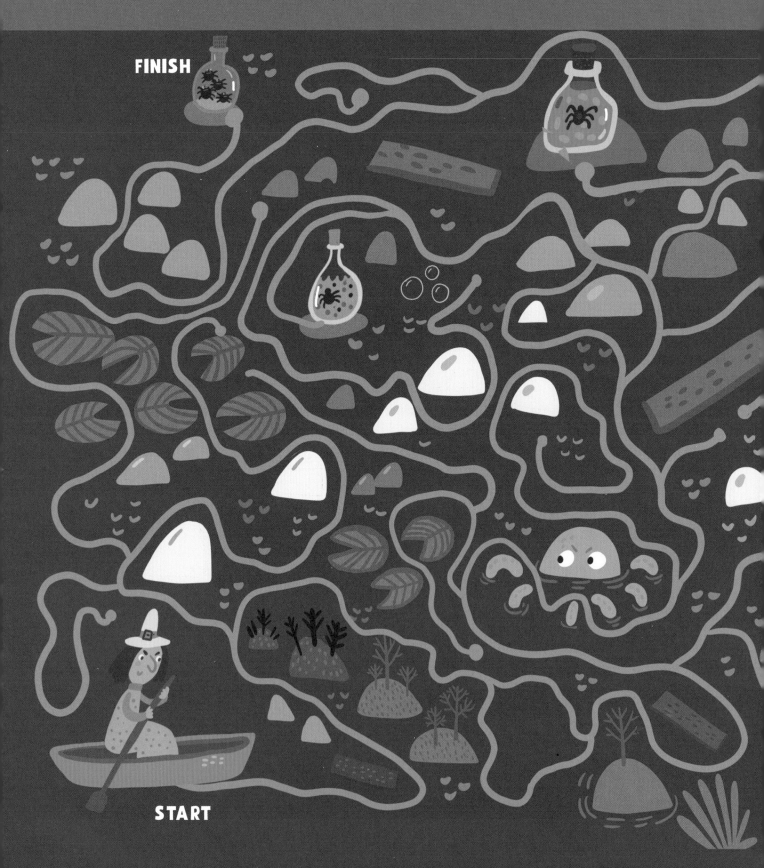

FINISH

START

Mushroom Maze

Help the baby spider find a way to Dad. Use the key at the bottom to find the correct path.

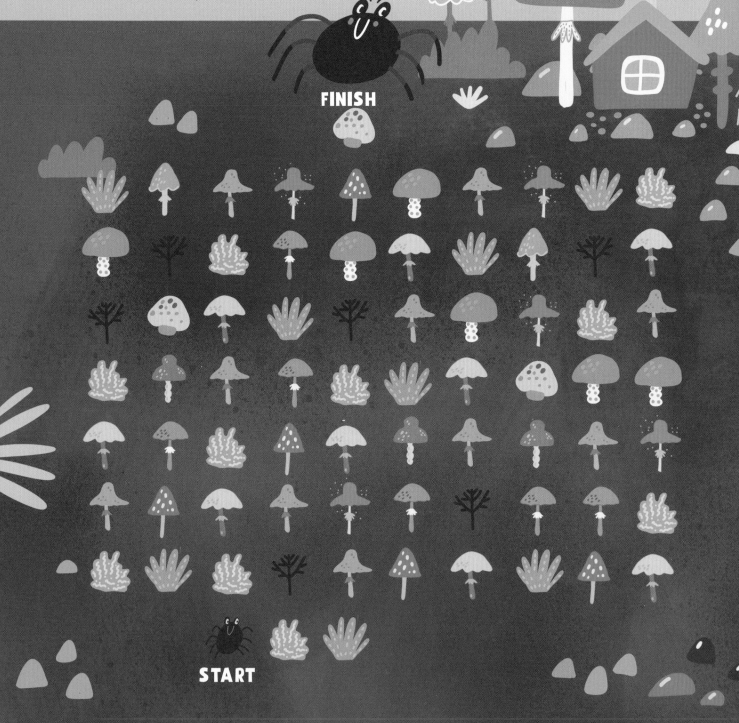

FINISH

START

Magic Leaf

The witch's cat is looking for the magic leaf. Can you help her find it? Watch out for the snakes and spiders!

Halloween Hunt

Can you guide the trick-or-treaters to the pumpkin?

START

FINISH

Snake Pit

Snakes have found their way into the witch's house! Help her find a path to the broom, but don't step on any snakes.

START

FINISH

Fix the Spaceship

Find a way for the alien to get to the top of the spaceship to fix it.

FINISH

START

Spooky Sweets

Follow the paths to find out what colors to use to color each treat.

Ghoulish Graveyard

Guide the witch through the cemetery maze and collect the pages from the book of spells.

FINISH

START

No Tricks, All Treats!

Follow each child's path to see
who got what candy.

Monsters!

Can you help each monster find its way home?

Martian Maze

The green alien with three eyes is sad! Can you find a path for the gray alien to take to cheer him up with a flower?

START

FINISH

Haunted Maze

Find a path from the castle to Octopus Lake. Be sure to step on all of the white rocks along the way!

FINISH

START

pyramid. Watch out for mummies, and don't step on any bones!

FINISH

START

Wicked Web

This spider wants to join his friends.
Find a path through the maze, and
pick up the dandelion seeds
along the way.

START

FINISH

Magic Potions

Follow each path to find out
what colors are in each potion.
Then color in the pictures!

Ghosts Galore

Help the ghost in the hat find its twin.

START

FINISH

Bonus: Find two ghosts wearing scarves.

Follow each ghost's path. Which one leads to the room in the house with the light on?

Secret Spell

To prepare the potion for the secret spell, follow the key to gather the ingredients in the correct order.

START →

FINISH

Haunting Hands

Help the wolf get to the gemstone.

FINISH

START

Peculiar Punch

In order to make the potion, gather the ingredients
in the correct order by following the key.

START

FINISH

Fall Harvest

Guide the hedgehog through the maze to the pile of yummy food.

START

FINISH

Sweet Treats

Help the mouse get to the candy that doesn't have a match.

START

FINISH

Pumpkin Patch

Help the boy find his way through the park to the pumpkin statue. Collect stars along the way, and watch out for spiders!

START

FINISH

Pick a Patch

Help the witch pick a patch for her hat.

Halloween Tricks

Can you figure out which path leads to which snack?

Skeleton Island

Help the skeleton get to the island to join his friends.

START

FINISH